Max and Little Bit's Big Adventure

by
Vera
Thornton

Max and Little Bit's Big Adventure

Written and Illustrated by
Vera Thornton

in memory of
Dad and Mom
Roy and Helen Thornton

inspired by
my
Family and Friends

and created for

my Beloved
Granddaughter
Morgan

Vera Thornton
15251 Eddy Lk. Rd.
Fenton, MI 48430-1608
(810) 629-6144
web: www.verathornton.com

Published by Comet Publishing
U.S.A.

Produced by David Kinder
Burton Printing Company/Comet Publishing
4270 S. Saginaw St.
Burton, MI 48529
(810) 742-3210
email: burtonprinting@sbcglobal.net

Printed in Hong Kong
Library of Congress Cataloging-in-Publication Data on file.
ISBN: 0-9753741-1-7

Max and Little Bit are best friends and do everything together if they can. Max is a Collie dog and Little Bit is a pony.

They don't look alike, but friends don't have to look alike to be friends do they?

And friends don't have to be the same size or shape! Little Bit and Max can tell you that!!

But they have a lot of fun together in the fields and forests on the farm.

They always stayed inside the yard and pastures and never wandered off.

But, ... one happy sunny day, when everything was nice and golden on the farm, they ran in happy circles and jumped and leaped until Little Bit jumped right over the fence.

Now, ... what should they do? Max was on one side and Little Bit was on the other. "Come back" Max barked. Little Bit said "Come over here." "Come with me Max! It's beautiful and we've never been here before. Max wasn't sure. They shouldn't go outside the fence. It was not a good idea. What should they do? ... It wouldn't take long and they would only stay a little while, ... what would it hurt?

So Max jumped over the fence and off they went looking at all the beautiful trees and colors. (that's not so bad, ... right?)

However, ... before long, they came to a big road with lots of cars. (and loud too!) They shouldn't cross the road. Max thought they should go back to the farm and into the pasture.

But Little Bit said, "Let's just run fast. We can cross, ... see all the grass on the other side? And maybe there are people with apples and carrots!!"

Max didn't want apples or carrots, he just wanted to go home, back where he was safe.

But, ... Little Bit ran fast across the road. Now Max was all alone.

55 MPH

So he ran across too.
"Let's go back?" Max barked.
Little Bit said, "Let's just stay a little while, then we'll go back!"
"Let's see what's over there."
Max saw many people selling lots of stuff.

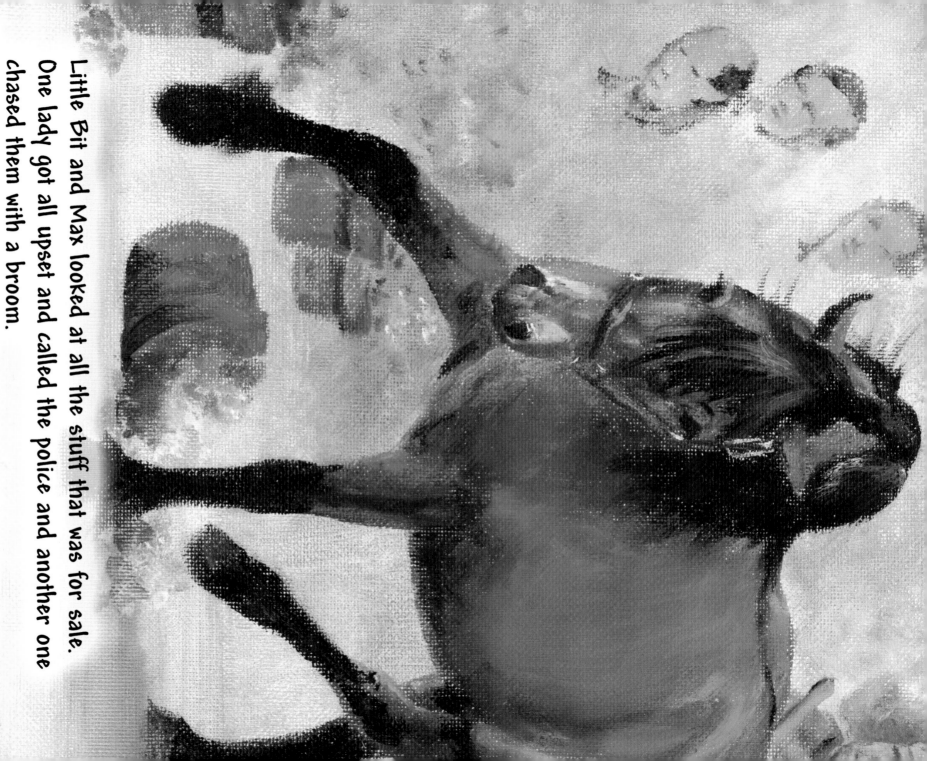

Little Bit and Max looked at all the stuff that was for sale. One lady got all upset and called the police and another one chased them with a broom.

Max and Little Bit just wanted to be friends but thought maybe they should leave. But where should they go??

Little Bit and Max walked and walked and walked and walked, not knowing what to do.

Max barked, "Let's go home!" But where was home?

They were lost!

A nice looking man came over to them and offered them a carrot and said, "Come with me, ... I'll help you!" And he had an apple, ... he looked friendly. "I'll take you home," he said in a friendly voice. "You can trust me!!"

Little Bit wanted the apple. He walked closer and reached for the apple. "No...!" Max barked. Max jumped and grabbed Little Bit's tail.

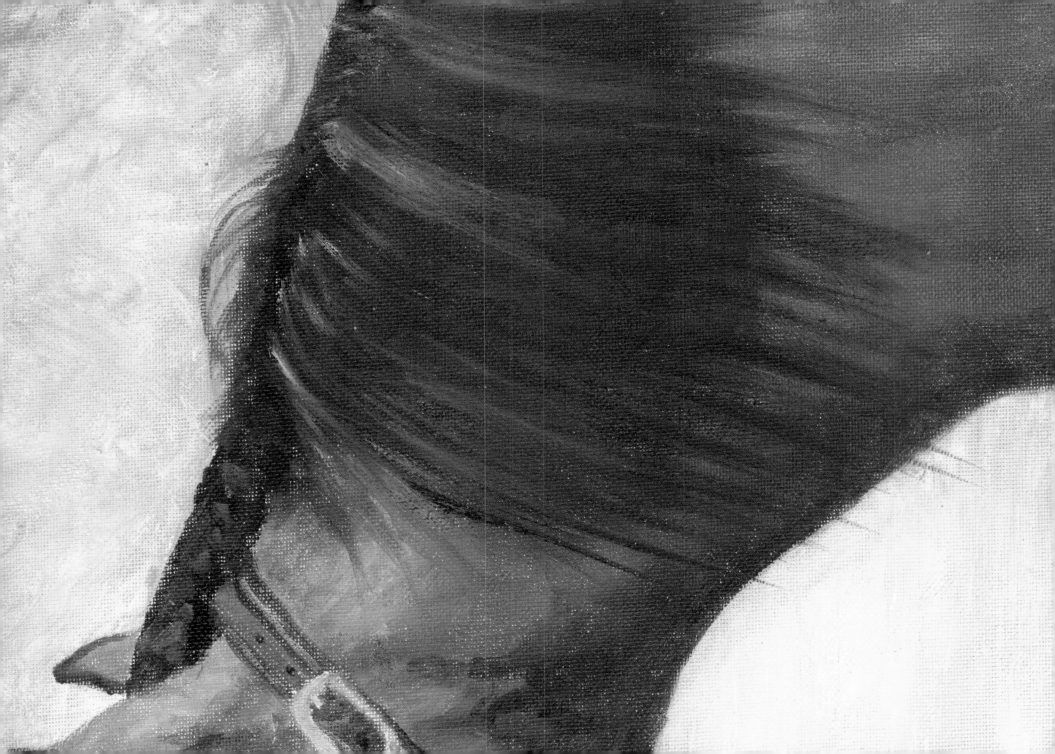

"Don't go with him, ... he's a stranger!!
Never go with strangers!!"
Little Bit and Max jumped back and started
to run away from the stranger.

...back past the upset ladies, ... back to the fast cars.
But how could they cross?
A voice came from behind them, "Come with me!
I'll help you, ... I'll take you home!!"

They turned to look. It was a policeman. "Come to me, I'll take you home!" he said again in a kind voice.

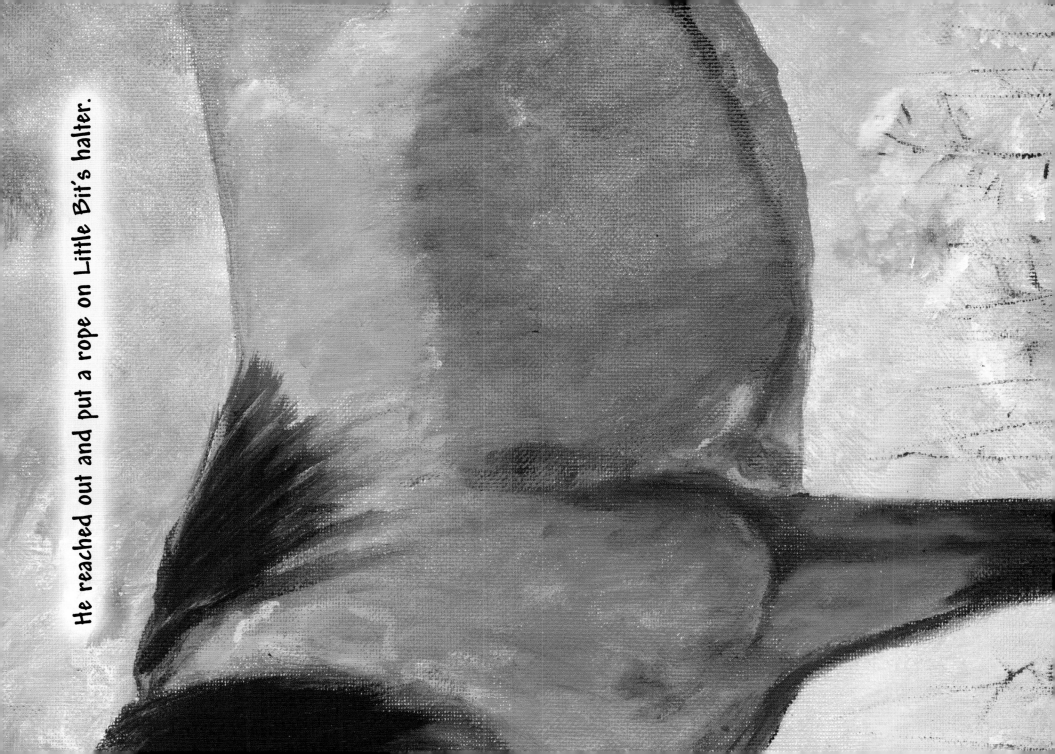

He reached out and put a rope on Little Bit's halter.

Then he stopped the cars and walked them safely across the road. Back through the woods, back to the farm, back to the pasture where they were safe, back to the barn.

Max was glad they didn't go with the stranger. Little Bit was glad he listened to his friend. They were really happy to be home and safe.

Some strangers look friendly,
but they are still strangers.
NEVER GO WITH
STRANGERS.
Friends take care of friends,
... friends play safe together.